EDNA

by Robert Burleigh

illustrated by Joanna Yardley

ORCHARD BOOKS • NEW YORK

This story is an imaginary re-creation of how Edna St. Vincent Millay, the great
American poet, may have written one of her most famous poems.

Orchard Books, A Grolier Company, 95 Madison Avenue, New York, NY 10016

"Recuerdo" by Edna St. Vincent Millay. From *Collected Poems*, HarperCollins. Copyright © 1922, 1950
by Edna St. Vincent Millay. All rights reserved. Reprinted by permission of Elizabeth Barnett, literary executor.

Manufactured in the United States of America. Printed and bound by Phoenix Color Corp.
Book design by Joanna Yardley and Mina Greenstein
The text of this book is set in 16 point Bernhard Modern BT.
The illustrations are gouache and pen and ink.
10 9 8 7 6 5 4 3 2 1

Library of Congress Cataloging-in-Publication Data
Burleigh, Robert. Edna / by Robert Burleigh ; illustrated by Joanna Yardley. p. cm.
Summary: Uses the imagined viewpoint of Edna St. Vincent Millay to re-create her early years
as a poet in New York City. Includes her poem "Recuerdo" and a brief profile of her life.
ISBN 0-531-30246-6 (trade : alk. paper)—ISBN 0-531-33246-2 (lib. : alk. paper)
1. Millay, Edna St. Vincent, 1892–1950—Juvenile fiction.
[1. Millay, Edna St. Vincent, 1892–1950—Fiction.
2. New York (N.Y.)—Fiction. 3. Poets—Fiction.]
I. Yardley, Joanna, ill.
II. Millay, Edna St. Vincent, 1892–1950.
Recuerdo. III. Title.
PZ7.B9244 Eg   2000
[Fic]—dc21   99-42667

NEW JERSEY

FERRY ROUTE

STATEN ISLAND

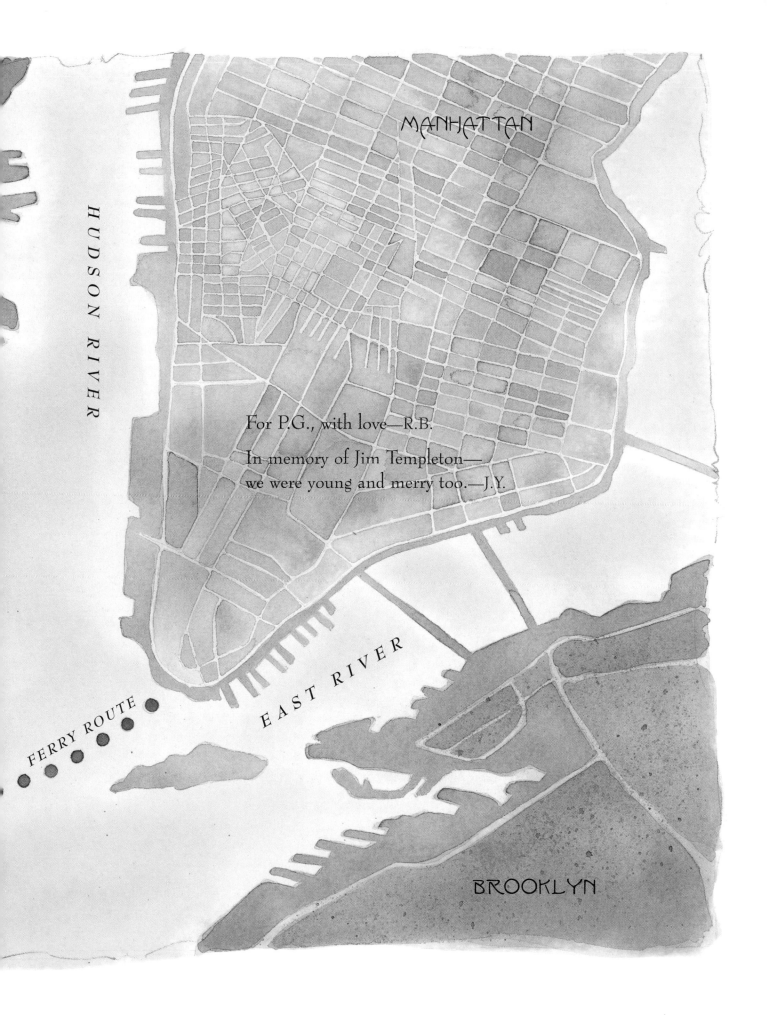

MANHATTAN

HUDSON RIVER

For P.G., with love—R.B.

In memory of Jim Templeton—
we were young and merry too.—J.Y.

EAST RIVER

FERRY ROUTE

BROOKLYN

Oh, how I love this great big city!
I love the crowds, I love the sounds, I love
the lights at night!

And I love my neighborhood too! It's called the Village. It's filled with lots and lots of little twisted streets that cross and recross and never seem to get anywhere. And it's special to me because so many poets and artists live here. And I am one of them!

From my apartment, I can see the far-off tall buildings, the laundry flapping on nearby roofs, and down below, the hurdy-gurdy man playing his organ and kids zipping by on roller skates. That's how I want to be too—free!

The Great War is ending, women are getting the vote, and it's a new America.

We don't have much money, my friends and I. I help
pay the rent by acting in small plays and selling my
poems to newspapers and magazines—when I can.

"It's spring here," I wrote to one editor, "and I'm
happy. Except I'm broke. Would you mind paying me
now instead of later?"

But we get by. We find cheap restaurants like Chumley's (a great dollar-dinner any night of the week) and Grand Ticino, a basement place where I sometimes sip tea and write all afternoon.

We go to free concerts, take long walks over the Brooklyn Bridge, and feel the wind on our faces. We ride the open, upper deck of a bus down Fifth Avenue, looking up at the big-windowed buildings and down at the policemen on their horses.

We hold parties, too, in this tiny apartment, where we huddle around the fireplace and read our work to one another. My friends laugh.
"Edna, stop waving your hands when you read!"
But they stop laughing and listen when they hear my poems. Some of my poems are about feelings I had just yesterday, and some of them are about my memories.

Once, a friend and I took the ferryboat from the tip of Manhattan to Staten Island. It was nighttime. The ferry went back and forth, back and forth. And you could ride it as often as you wished!

The ride made me feel peaceful. I watched the white foam billow in the boat's wake. I leaned out and listened to the buoy bells—*gong, gong, gong, gong*—in the watery dark.

The boat churned right past the Statue of
Liberty. We stood on the deck and laughed
and waved at the huge bronze lady.
The boat wasn't fancy. Not at all! If we
wanted to sit, there were some rough old
wooden seats that looked like church pews.
I even smelled the hay for the horses
that the ferry sometimes carried!
But we didn't care.

Then one of us had an idea. *Let's get off and walk
on Staten Island.* So we did!
We climbed up one of the high, grassy hills.
From there, we gazed out on the distant, blinking
lights—hundreds and hundreds of them—from
the windows of New York's giant skyscrapers.
At the same time, far down in the
darkness, we could hear the ghostly
whistles and lonely horns of the boats
and ships in the harbor.

We had a bag of fruit with us. I nibbled on a pear
and pulled my cape over my shoulders. It was chilly,
but it felt good sitting there on the hillside, looking
and listening and talking.

The sky in the east slowly began to lighten, and the sun rose up over the gray water. We had stayed out all night!

At last, we hiked down to the ferry and came back.

Did you ever feel so happy that it made you do some crazy, funny thing? Back in the city, we bought a newspaper from an old woman. Then we looked at each other. *Hey, why not?* We gave her everything—our apples, our pears, and most of the little money we had!

We kept just enough to get home on the subway. . . .

But the story of the ferryboat ride doesn't end there. Last night, I was sitting at my desk. Suddenly a poem started to come to me.

It was as if that night had stayed for a long time inside me, like a seed. And now it was sprouting. It all welled up—the sights, the sounds, the feelings.

And I wrote it down. I call my poem "Recuerdo" because my friend was from Latin America and *recuerdo* means "remembrance" in Spanish. I hope he reads it someday and remembers.

I hope he remembers how it was—living in the world's greatest city, being young, and caring for nothing but to be alive here and now. And maybe my poem will make you think of a time in your life when you were "very tired and very merry" too.

Recuerdo

We were very tired, we were very merry—
We had gone back and forth all night on the ferry.
It was bare and bright, and smelled like a stable—
But we looked into a fire, we leaned across a table,
We lay on a hill-top underneath the moon;
And the whistles kept blowing, and the dawn came soon.

We were very tired, we were very merry—
We had gone back and forth all night on the ferry;
And you ate an apple, and I ate a pear,
From a dozen of each we had bought somewhere;
And the sky went wan, and the wind came cold,
And the sun rose dripping, a bucketful of gold.

We were very tired, we were very merry,
We had gone back and forth all night on the ferry.
We hailed, "Good morrow, mother!" to a shawl-covered head,
And bought a morning paper, which neither of us read;
And she wept, "God bless you!" for the apples and pears,
And we gave her all our money but our subway fares.

Afterword

Edna St. Vincent Millay, born in 1892, is one of America's best-known and most-loved poets. She grew up in the seacoast town of Camden, Maine, where she loved to play with her two sisters. Early on, she showed a talent for acting and writing. Although her family was somewhat poor, Edna was able to go to college through the kindness of a woman who heard Edna read her poem "Renascence" and decided to help raise money for the young poet's education.

Edna moved to New York at a time when fashions were changing, women were getting the vote, and a new freedom to experiment was everywhere in the air. In this atmosphere, she bloomed and quickly became known for her creativity and independence. (Her close friends often called her "Vincent.") She wrote about falling in love, about music, and about the passage of time. "Recuerdo" was written during these years. Some of her other well-known poems are "Spring," "Afternoon on a Hill," "The Buck in the Snow," "What Lips My Lips Have Kissed," and "First Fig," with its famous opening line: "My candle burns at both ends." Edna received numerous honors and prizes for her books of poetry. She died in 1950 at the age of fifty-eight.